A NOTE TO PARENTS

When your children are ready to "step into reading," giving them the right books—and lots of them—is as crucial as giving them the right food to eat. **Step into Reading Books** present exciting stories and information reinforced with lively, colorful illustrations that make learning to read fun, satisfying, and worthwhile. They are priced so that acquiring an entire library of them is affordable. And they are beginning readers with an important difference—they're written on four levels.

   Step 1 Books, with their very large type and extremely simple vocabulary, have been created for the very youngest readers. **Step 2 Books** are both longer and slightly more difficult. **Step 3 Books,** written to mid-second-grade reading levels, are for the child who has acquired even greater reading skills. **Step 4 Books** offer exciting nonfiction for the increasingly proficient reader.

Library of Congress Cataloging in Publication Data:
Lerner, Sharon. Big Bird says—. (Step into Reading. A Step 1 book) SUMMARY: Sesame Street
Muppet characters play a game in which they obey commands from Big Bird.
    1. Children's stories, American.   [1. Games—Fiction.   2. Puppets—Fiction.   3. Stories
in rhyme]   I. Mathieu, Joseph, ill.   II. Title.   III. Series.   PZ8.3.L5493Bh   1985
[E]   85-1959   ISBN: 0-394-87499-4 (trade); 0-394-97499-9 (lib. bdg.)

Manufactured in the United States of America   12   13   14   15

STEP INTO READING is a trademark of Random House, Inc.

Step into Reading

Big Bird Says...

A Game to Read and Play

Featuring Jim Henson's Sesame Street Muppets

by Sharon Lerner

illustrated by Joe Mathieu

A Step 1 Book

Random House/Children's Television Workshop

I know a game called
"Big Bird Says"
I'd like to play
with you.
Just follow me
and read along.
I'll tell you
what to do.

Big Bird says

to touch your nose.

Shut your eyes.

Then touch your toes.

Touch the top
of someone's head.

Touch someone
who is in bed.

Brush your teeth
and wash your face.

Put on your shoe
and tie your lace.

Big Bird says
to touch the floor.

Put on your coat.

Go out the door.

Pull a wagon.

Bounce a ball.

Walk on stilts
five feet tall.

Find a girl.

Then a boy.

Share your very
favorite toy.

Big Bird says

to catch a goose.

Find someone
whose tooth is loose.

Find something
that makes you lucky.

Touch something
you think is yucchy.

Pat a dog.

Then pat a cat.

Kiss someone
who wears a hat.

Big Bird says
to say bow-wow.

Quack like a duck.

Moo like a cow.

Jump way up high
and flap your wing.

Stand on your head
and start to sing.

Draw a picture
of a clown.

Now do the same thing
upside down.

Touch your elbow.

Then your knee.

I'll tickle you.

You tickle me.

I'd love to play some more with you, but now YOU tell ME what to do!